RF

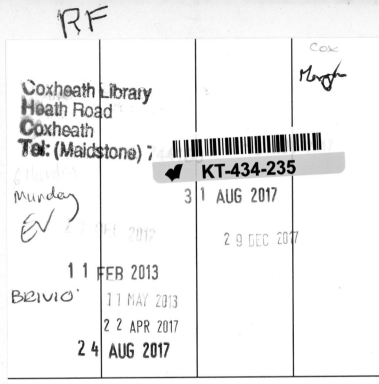
Please return on or before the latest date above.
You can renew online at *www.kent.gov.uk/libs*
or by telephone 08458 247 200

_____

_____

CUSTOMER SERVICE EXCELLENCE

Libraries & Archives

Kent
County
Council

00884\DTP\RN\07.07   LIB 7

HERE COMES THE BRIDE

Isobel's sister is getting married and wants her to be a bridesmaid. How hard can it be? Very hard, it seems, as bride-to-be, Kelly, lurches from one disaster to the next. Isobel tries to help, but her own relationship is threatened, her beloved granddad ends up in hospital, and then she has a car accident. She begins to wonder if the wedding will ever take place — and if she would be in any condition to be a bridesmaid . . .

KAT PARKHURST

HERE COMES THE BRIDE

Complete and Unabridged

LINFORD
Leicester

First published in Great Britain in 2002

First Linford Edition
published 2011

British Library CIP Data

Parkhurst, Kat.
  Here comes the bride. - -
  (Linford romance library)
  1. Weddings- -Planning- -Fiction.
  2. Bridesmaids- -Fiction.
  3. Love stories. 4. Large type books.
  I. Title II. Series
  823.9'2–dc22

  ISBN 978–1–4448–0895–7

Published by
F. A. Thorpe (Publishing)
Anstey, Leicestershire

Set by Words & Graphics Ltd.
Anstey, Leicestershire
Printed and bound in Great Britain by
T. J. International Ltd., Padstow, Cornwall

This book is printed on acid-free paper

1

'Isobel, I've got some bad news.'

'What sort of bad news?' I clutched the phone to my ear. 'Not about the wedding?'

'Sort of about the wedding, but I can't tell you on the phone. Can you come round?'

'Well, yes, I suppose so. Do you mean now?'

'Pretty soonish. I've got to go and pick up the cake.'

I glanced at Grandad, who was sitting opposite me at the kitchen table drinking a cappuccino, the creamy bits of which had given him an extra moustache. It couldn't be that bad, I thought, if she was still picking up the cake. Not so bad that it was cancelled or anything.

'See you in a bit.' I put down the phone and said in answer to Grandad's raised eyebrows, 'Kelly. She says she's got bad news about the wedding.'

He wiped froth from his moustache with a finger. 'I shouldn't worry too much, love. Your sister's probably being a drama puss again.'

'Don't you mean a drama queen?'

He grinned. 'Whatever. So what does she want you to do? Go round there?'

'Yes. Shall I drop you back on the way?'

'No, you're all right. The walk will do me good.' He stood up, pressing a hand to his back. 'It'll straighten out the creases.'

I smiled at him. 'It's very stressful arranging a wedding, you know.'

'Stressful for everyone around her.' His blue eyes twinkled behind his glasses. 'You go and sort her out and give me a ring later.'

'You don't have to rush off. Stay and have another coffee, if you like.'

'I can't make it like you can. No, I'll get going.'

Grandad could make a pretty mean

cappuccino, I thought, frowning. More likely he'd decided not to stay because he could never find anything in my kitchen.

'If you kept everything in the same place, it wouldn't be a problem,' he often said. I sometimes wondered if his eyes were worse than he let on, but although I often nagged him to go to the opticians and get some stronger glasses, he wouldn't have it.

'No point,' he'd say. 'You expect your eyes to wear out when you get to my age. I like the glasses I've got. They make me look distinguished, don't you think? Besides,' he'd add, 'the world looks perfectly fine to me.'

That, I thought as I drove round to my sister's, was probably because he reinvented it. Drama puss was a perfect description for Kelly. Tall, blonde and exuberant, there was always some drama going on in her life, especially since she'd announced she was getting married. I was more like our mum. I'd inherited brown hair, short legs and a

3

sensible outlook on life, but the envy I'd felt towards my sister when we were kids had levelled out into an amused affection now that we were both in our thirties.

I'd been pleased when she said she was marrying Tim. Pleased that at last she was getting some sort of stability into her life. Maybe my relief had been slightly premature, I thought wryly. Since she'd announced the date, there'd been no end of problems. Twice she'd called the whole thing off because it was just soooo stressful. I'd sat in her flat while she ran her fingers through her streaked blonde hair and managed to cry buckets without smudging her beautifully made-up eyes.

I wondered what it would be this time. Something to do with the seating arrangements probably. One or another of her equally volatile friends announcing that they couldn't possibly sit with each other. Seating arrangements had been causing problems the last time I'd seen her.

4

'Thank God you're here, Isobel.' She flung her arms around me as soon as I walked in and I was suffocated with perfume. 'I'm at my wits' end. I just don't know how I'm going to sort out this one.'

'Calm down and tell me what's happened.' She did look worried, I thought, with a little jolt of unease.

Do you want a coffee? No, actually you're going to need something stronger when I tell you what's happened.'

'It's only eleven o clock,' I pointed out.

'There's wine on the table.' She ushered me through with a wave of her elegant fingers. A bottle of red and two glasses sat amid a pile of black and gold place name cards on the glass coffee table.

'These are nice.' I picked one up. Looked like I'd been right about the latest problem.

'Yes. Look, Isobel, I don't really know how to tell you this.'

'Just tell me.' I moved a pile of

5

ironing off the couch and sat down.

She perched on the chair opposite me, crossing her long legs. 'It's Dad. He's given me an ultimatum.'

'Ultimatum?' I frowned. 'What are you talking about?'

'He says he's not coming to the wedding if Dave does.'

I stared at her. 'Dave? You mean my Dave?'

She nodded. 'I'm really sorry, but you know what Dad's like when he's got a bee in his bonnet.' She poured wine and handed me a glass.

I took it unthinkingly. 'So what's brought this on?'

'Well, you have to admit they've never seen eye to eye, have they?'

That was certainly true. My dad and my significant other had got off on the wrong foot from the minute they'd met. Dad had taken one look at Dave's spiky bleached hair and tattooed arms and scowled, and Dave, aware of his disapproval, had gone into defensive mode. He'd then proceeded to drink far too much, which hadn't impressed my teetotal father one bit. Dave had tried to redeem himself on subsequent occasions, but they'd never really hit it off. Sometimes I thought they were just too different. Dad was as middle-of-the-road as you could get, while Dave was so far off the proverbial beaten track that he was in danger of getting lost. Even so, I was shocked to discover that Dad felt strongly enough to come out with something like this.

'It's a bit late in the day to start issuing ultimatums, isn't it?' I sipped the wine. 'Why didn't he say something before?'

'I don't know.' She blinked a couple of times and went slightly pink, and I had the feeling she knew more than she was telling me. 'He and Tim went out for a drink last week and he mentioned it then.'

'Did he say why?'

'Er, no, not really.'

'But you're getting married in a fortnight.'

She hugged her arms around herself. 'Don't be cross with me, Izzy. We can still sort it out, can't we? I mean, couldn't Dave just say he wasn't feeling too good on the day or something, and not turn up? That would keep everybody happy, wouldn't it?'

'No, it wouldn't.' I put my wine glass on the table with a clink and stood up. 'It wouldn't keep me happy for a start.'

'Where are you going?'

I strode to the window and looked out at the rather uninspiring view over Pepperbox Close. Washing lines stretched across grey gardens that were layered with a mulch of autumn leaves from all the rain we'd had.

'Izzy, don't make a big thing about it. Please. Dave wouldn't mind not coming to the wedding, would he? It's only a couple of hours.'

I didn't say anything. For the last five months or so, Dave had been as involved in the trials and tribulations of my sister's wedding as I had. Not to mention the fact that we were paying for her honeymoon as a surprise wedding present. Our rent and bills took up most of our wages. Dave ran a landscape gardening business. Lately he'd been putting in even more hours than usual so we could afford the honeymoon.

I pictured myself telling him he wasn't welcome and knew I couldn't. Dave might look like a bit of a hard nut on the outside, but I knew better. He was an orphan and he'd been brought up in the kind of children's home where attack had been the best means of defence. It wasn't a background that had equipped him for dealing with tricky family situations and my dad had always been a bit on the tricky side. If I told him he wasn't welcome at Kelly's wedding, he'd pretend he didn't care, but deep down I knew he'd be hurt. Crushed.

'I'd mind if he didn't come,' I said quietly. 'In fact, I'd go as far as to say that if he doesn't come, I'm not coming either.'

'But you've got to.' Kelly sounded genuinely shocked. 'You're my maid of honour. You're my sister. I'd go to pieces if you weren't there.'

A part of my mind registered that being her sister was obviously a secondary consideration and I felt a little spark of anger growing inside me, heating up into something dangerous. I turned round to face her. 'You're going to have to sort this out with Dad,' I said. 'You can't un-invite Dave now. He's got as much right to be there as I have.'

She'd gone a bit white, I saw, but the shock on her face only strengthened my resolve.

'If you're not going to talk to Dad,' I added, feeling the beginnings of a headache, 'then I will. I'll phone him up tonight and find out why he's being so unreasonable.'

She bit her lip. 'Please don't say anything, Izzy. It'll only make things worse. Look, I'll try to talk to him again. Just give me a few days.'

I still had a headache when I got home just after two. Kelly had to be exaggerating about Dad's attitude, I thought, although I couldn't for the life of me think why. True, our father had always been awkward. He hadn't inherited any of Grandad's laid-back attitude to life. His world was black and white. You were in the right or you were in the wrong. Generally, that translated into him being in the right and whoever he was arguing with being in the wrong. Dad had been a maths teacher before he retired. He'd been the old-fashioned type of teacher, believing in strict discipline and respect, ruling his classes with a rod of iron. He hadn't mellowed with age, either. Mum sometimes laughingly said that if anything he'd got worse since he'd stopped teaching.

'He misses having someone to boss around, love,' she said, if I ever pointed out that he treated everyone around him as if they were his pupils. 'Just

11

humour him. It's easier that way.'

Now I came to think of it, there'd been a problem the last time he and Dave had met, which had been at my Aunt Beatrice's funeral in February. Nothing major, just a difference of opinion on suitable attire for the occasion. Dave had come straight from work and had still been wearing his baseball cap. He'd taken it off in church but put it back on for sandwiches in the pub afterwards, and Dad had made a beeline for him.

I cleared up the coffee cups from earlier and tried to remember what had actually been said. It didn't make a lot of sense. I knew Dad was stubborn, but not wanting Dave at the wedding because of his dress sense was a bit over the top, even for my father.

I glanced at my watch. Dave had started at six this morning, even though it was Saturday. More overtime, I thought bitterly, to buy a present for a wedding he wasn't welcome at. Charming! I didn't often get angry — that was

Kelly's prerogative — but I was pretty angry now. I put on a load of washing, paced the kitchen, vacuumed the front room, then paced a bit more. Then I decided to phone Grandad. He'd always been the only one of the family who Dad paid any attention to. Mind you, he had the advantage of being able to remember him in short trousers.

He listened patiently and I imagined him sitting in his favourite room, the conservatory, where he kept the phone because he said it was the only place in the house light enough to see the numbers without his glasses.

'I didn't think your father had that much of a problem with Dave,' he said at last. 'Are you sure Kelly hasn't got her wires crossed?'

'She sounded pretty sure. She said Dad had given her an ultimatum.'

'Well, I know they had words at Aunt Beatrice's funeral, God rest her soul, but if he was still brooding on that, he'd have said something. Do you want me to have a word?'

'No,' I said, 'let Kelly have another go first. If that doesn't work, I'll ask Mum. I'll speak to Dave when he comes in.'

'Speak to me about what?' Dave said from the doorway, and I jumped.

'Hello, love, I didn't hear you come in. I thought you were working all day.'

'Job didn't take as long as I thought.' He grinned. 'What's up? Catch you talking to your secret lover, did I?'

'No, he called earlier.' I put down the phone. 'You'll have to try harder than that to catch me out.'

Still grinning, he took his baseball cap off and put it on the table, and I found myself staring at it distractedly.

'So what did you want to talk to me about?' He got a packet of crisps out of the cupboard. 'I'm starving. Have you had anything?'

'A glass of wine with Kelly,' I said, and he stopped in his tracks and looked at me. 'She asked me round. She had a few problems. About you, actually.'

'Oh?' His voice was guarded, and I went on hastily, 'Nothing serious. You

14

know how she makes mountains out of molehills.'

He came back to the table and sat down. 'What has she said?' He sounded so worried that I felt guilty. I couldn't tell him about Dad's ultimatum. Knowing Dave, he'd just say he wouldn't go. I meant what I'd said to Kelly: it was both of us or nothing. And if neither of us went, it would cause the sort of rift between Dave and my family that would be impossible to heal. I decided to try a different tack.

'Er, Dave, you know at Aunt Beatrice's funeral when Dad went off on one about your baseball cap? Well, can you remember what was said?'

He opened the packet of crisps and looked at me. 'Only what I told you at the time. He said that it showed a lack of respect. I told him that respect was something you felt, not something you wore. Just because you wore a fancy suit didn't mean you were any more respectful — far from it.'

I groaned, and he frowned.

'Isobel, you're starting to worry me.' He finished his crisps, scrunched the packet into a ball and missed the bin. 'Just tell me what's going on.'

'Oh, nothing,' I murmured. 'I think Dad's just being oversensitive about what everyone's wearing at the wedding.'

He stood up, went and retrieved the crisp packet and flicked it into the bin. 'I know he's your father, but he needs to lighten up a bit.' He came back to the table and leant on the back of the chair he'd just been sitting on. 'You know what his trouble is, don't you? Everyone backs down to him. You, your mum and Kelly. You all tiptoe around him like he's some sort of god or something. No wonder he acts like he does.' Irritation darkened his brown eyes until they were almost black and he added, 'He ought to be making sure Kelly's relaxed about her big day, not winding her up.'

I didn't answer. Deep down, I knew

he had a point. We did all tiptoe around Dad.

I sighed and Dave straightened up. 'I'll make us a coffee.' With his back to me, he said, 'I'm sorry, that was uncalled for. Let's face it, what do I know about family politics?'

'It's all right.' I felt even worse now. Dave had always been cagey about his past. If he couldn't make a joke of it, like the fact he was glad he'd been left in a carrier bag outside Dave's Chippy and not at Ebenezer's Antiques next door, then he didn't tell me at all. There was a lot of stuff I knew he'd never tell me.

I went across and hugged him from behind. 'I'm sorry too. You're right. Dad is difficult, but I'm worried about the wedding, that's all.'

'It'll be fine,' he said, twisting round and putting his hands on my shoulders. 'I'll stay out of his way if that'll help. There'll be lots of other people there. It shouldn't be difficult.'

Now definitely wasn't the time to tell

17

him Dad was refusing to go at all if he did, I thought, resting my head against his shoulder and breathing in the familiar outdoor smell of his skin. I was going to have to find some other way around this.

* * *

Three days later I was no nearer to a solution. I'd phoned Kelly twice to ask what was happening and she just said she hadn't had a chance to speak to Dad yet.

'You're going to have to speak to him soon,' I told her.

'Yes, all right,' she snapped. 'But I have got rather a lot of other stuff to organise, you know.'

I could have phoned Mum, I suppose, but I was still trying to convince myself that the whole thing would blow over if I ignored it. For a while I'd toyed with the idea of asking Tim what had been said when he'd gone out with my father, but I was pretty sure he wouldn't tell me. Tim was a nice bloke, but he tended to be a bit overprotective of my sister and I sometimes got the feeling he didn't approve of Dave either. The previous Saturday we'd bumped into him in the shop where we were hiring the men's suits and he'd seemed a bit cool. Not hostile exactly, but definitely offish towards Dave.

On Tuesday evening I popped in to see Grandad on my way home from my shift at the nursing home. We sat in his conservatory and discussed things. He'd had the conservatory added on to the back of the house two years after we'd lost Gran and it was a beautiful place. All hanging plants and cane furniture, although not just your average conservatory furniture. Grandad had splashed out on a cane chair that had some sort of roller effect, so that it moved under the slightest touch. It was a sort of cross between a rocking-chair and a swinging seat and was wonderfully relaxing to sit in. At the moment I was sitting in it and, what with the evening sunlight slanting through the glass onto my face and the motion of the chair, I was starting to drift off.

'The thing is, we're all going out on Friday night, aren't we?' Grandad said. 'So we can clear the air then.'

'Friday night?' Adrenaline snapped open my eyes. 'Are we?'

'A family get together instead of a hen night. Didn't Kelly mention it? She's booked a table at that place around the corner from her with the pagoda.'

I was briefly distracted by an image of a restaurant with a temple outside, before I realised he meant pergola. 'She didn't say anything,' I said.

Grandad winked at me. 'Probably just slipped her mind.'

'Maybe we're not invited.' I sat up in the chair and it rocked a little harder. I could feel the peace slipping away like the last of the sun's rays.

''Course you're invited. Just turn up. If there's any problem, we can get it

20

sorted out then, can't we?'

'Yes, I suppose we can.'

'I spoke to your father earlier. He's picking me up on the way through. Everything will be fine, don't worry.'

His air of confidence was reassuring. I just hoped it wasn't misplaced.

★　★　★

As we got ready to go out on Friday night, I could feel my stomach churning, but while Dave was quieter than usual, he didn't seem to have any misgivings about the coming evening. Probably because he didn't know the full story, I thought guiltily.

'I've even washed this,' he said, twirling his baseball cap in his fingers as I did my hair at the dressing table.

'Dave! You're not?' I felt the heat gathering in my neck and he grinned.

'I'm kidding.' He put his arms around me. 'I don't deliberately go out to wind him up, you know. Anyway, it wouldn't go with my suit.' He threw the cap on to our bed and straightened his black leather tie. 'Don't look so worried. By the end of the evening, all this nonsense will be sorted out.'

We were the last to arrive. As we went beneath the trellis of plants that hung around the restaurant entrance, I could see my family standing at the bar. Mum and Dad had their backs to me and Tim was ordering drinks. None of them looked particularly dressed up. Kelly was wearing a denim jacket over black jeans, her blonde hair pinned up in a way that looked casual but that I knew took her ages to achieve. Tim wore cords and Dad looked like he'd got a tracksuit on.

Suddenly I felt uneasy and over-dressed. I'd made Dave put on his suit, thinking it might help his case with Dad, but now I was beginning to regret it. Dave looked uncomfortable as well, I thought. Still, it was too late now.

'Hi, everybody,' I said cheerily.

Grandad winked and Mum gave me a tired smile. 'Hello, love. You haven't been round to see us lately. How are you?'

Dad turned around slowly, saw Dave and stiffened. Then he looked him up and down. His blue eyes were cold and his lips, thin at the best of times, were compressed into a hard line. His hostility was so intense it was almost tangible. Beside me, Dave, sensitive as radar where other people's opinions of him were concerned, took an involuntary step backwards. Kelly gave me a helpless glance and, at her side, Tim looked embarrassed.

'Nice to see you both,' Grandad said easily, stepping forward so that he stood between Dave and my father. 'Nice touch, that tie. Is it leather?'

Dave glanced at him and Tim said quickly, 'What are you two drinking?' The tension dissipated. Dad turned away to say something to Mum, but beside me I could feel that Dave was rigid with apprehension. I couldn't blame him either, I thought. If it hadn't been for the fact that I didn't want to ruin Kelly's evening, I would have said we should go, although Grandad did have a point. Tonight was probably our best chance of getting to the bottom of whatever was bothering Dad.

He and Dave sat at opposite ends of the table, but that didn't improve the atmosphere much. Mum hardly spoke through our starter. Even Grandad looked worried and I realised that, for once in her life, Kelly hadn't been exaggerating. Dad really did have a problem with Dave and, with just over a week to go to the wedding, I couldn't leave it like this any longer.

When Mum went to the bathroom in the break before our main course, I followed her. 'What on earth's got into Dad?' I said, as she dried her hands on a green paper towel.

'What do you mean?'

'Kelly said he didn't want Dave at the wedding, but I thought she was just making mountains out of molehills. She obviously isn't, though. What's going on?'

24

She looked at me, a faint pink flush spreading across her cheeks, and didn't say anything.

'Is it the row at Aunt Beatrice's funeral? Over Dave's baseball cap?'

'His baseball cap?' She looked startled.

'Only I'd have thought Dad would have said something before now. Issuing ultimatums at the last minute is a bit much, isn't it? Even for him.'

She blinked a couple of times and started to edge towards the door. 'I told Kelly she should have said something earlier.'

There was a desperation in her voice that seemed way out of context. I was beginning to get the impression I was missing something important.

Behind her the door swung open and Kelly came into the cloakroom. 'What are you two conflabbing about?' She glanced at our mother. 'Anything I should know about?'

'I think you know the answer to that, don't you?' Mum said ambiguously, then fled before either of us could stop her.

I looked at my sister's face in the mirror. 'Mum seems to think Dad's got some rock-solid reason for not wanting Dave at your wedding. So either she's going as doolally as he is, or there's some big secret that no one wants to tell me about.'

Kelly didn't answer straight away. She rummaged in her handbag, produced a pink lipstick and began to reapply it.

'Well?' I said irritably. 'Don't keep me in suspense.'

'Actually, it's not just Dad who doesn't want him there.' She didn't look at me. 'I'm not keen either.'

I could feel my cheeks begin to burn. 'Why exactly don't any of you want my boyfriend to come? Is it because he's not as conventional as we are? Is that it? Some kind of snobbery thing, for heaven's sake?'

'It's not as simple as that, no.' She put the lipstick back in her bag and met my eyes in the mirror. 'Look, Isobel, I didn't want to tell you this, but I think I'm going to have to.'

I could feel a little shock of coldness beginning inside me. Go on.'

'Dave and I . . . well, we . . . ' She frowned. 'We had a bit of a fling.'

For a moment everything in the room seemed to spin. Then it stilled and a long way off I heard my sister's voice. 'It didn't mean anything, Izzy. Obviously, or I wouldn't be marrying Tim next week, would I?'

I blinked. Somewhere inside me the coldness was turning into a sick feeling, spreading through my body. It was even affecting my hands, I realised. They were trembling, moving of their own accord. Kelly's face in the mirror looked distorted.

I closed my eyes and my mind conjured up a brief, Technicolor image of her and Dave in bed together. I pictured him cupping her face in his hands as he did to me. Pictured his traitorous fingers moving over her flawless skin.

I remembered when I'd first introduced him to my sister. I'd left it ages because I'd been worried that once he saw her, he wouldn't want to settle for short, brown-haired and sensible. He'd be beguiled by blonde hair and sparkle. In the event it hadn't happened. Looking back, he'd seemed quite unimpressed with her — almost dismissive, despite the fact that she'd flirted unashamedly with him all evening.

'Don't you fancy her at all?' I'd asked him later on, hating myself for voicing my insecurities but desperate to know.

'I'm not into drama queens,' he'd said, smiling, and I remembered loving him for his perception. Most people found Kelly enchanting when they first met her. They didn't see the flip side of the glitter. They only found out later about her fickleness, her impatience, and by then it was usually too late. They'd already fallen for her.

I wondered bitterly whether Dave's indifference had just hidden his real feelings. It must have done, or we wouldn't be having this conversation now.

'Izzy, you haven't heard a word I've said. Don't just stand there like you've seen a ghost. It's no big deal, you know.'

Her voice cracked into my thoughts and I felt something snap inside me. It might not be a big deal to her — she could get a boyfriend with a click of her manicured fingers — but Dave was the only man I'd ever really trusted. Really fallen head over heels in love with.

'I don't want to hear your excuses,' I shouted, pain searing through me as I reached for the door and yanked it open.

'Come back! I haven't . . . ' Her words were lost as the door slammed behind me and I ran back out into the restaurant. As I rushed between the tables, nearly knocking a waiter flying in my frantic haste to get away, I wondered how everything could still look so normal. How could everyone

29

still be sitting there, laughing and drinking and winding spaghetti round their forks, when the world was crashing down around us?

I didn't have to pass the table where my family sat as I charged towards the door, which was just as well. I didn't think I could bear to see Dave's face when he realised I knew his secret. I couldn't believe that I had been so utterly and completely wrong about him. It was only as I ran out of the restaurant door into the darkening street, past the rain misting in the light of the street lamps, that I realised the world wasn't crashing down. Well, theirs wasn't anyway. It was only my world that was crashing down. Only my world that had shattered into irreparable fragments.

2

It wasn't until I'd run to the end of the block and turned the corner and the restaurant was no longer in sight that I stopped to think. Now, standing on the pavement, my hair getting wetter in the fine mist of rain, rationality was beginning to creep back into my mind. I couldn't wander the streets all night. I wasn't dressed for it. I was dressed, I thought, with a little sigh of irony, for a comfy sit-down meal with my family to celebrate my sister's forthcoming wedding. Not for running away.

Again I saw Kelly's face in the mirror, heard her voice saying, 'It's no big deal, Izzy. It was just a fling.'

What was a fling, anyway? A kiss, maybe, when they'd both drunk too much? My heart sped up again. Even the thought of them kissing sent my stomach into knots, but it was bearable.

I could cope with a kiss. What I couldn't cope with was the fact that Dave hadn't told me.

He was always polite to my sister, but there'd never been anything more in his attitude. Sometimes I'd got the feeling he was a little irritated by her. Could Kelly possibly be lying about them having a fling? No, that was crazy. She'd know I'd only have to talk to him to confirm things — and while my sister might be fond of plumping things up a bit in the interests of being the centre of attention, I didn't think she'd actually lie about something like that.

Something was nagging at the corner of my mind. I walked a bit further along the street and then I remembered the conversation I'd had with Dave last Saturday. That sudden, guarded expression when I'd mentioned Kelly had a problem concerning him. I was starting to feel sick again. And I was getting wetter. In my hurry to get out of the restaurant, I hadn't picked up my jacket.

There was a taxi rank just ahead of me. I would go round to Grandad's, I decided. He would still be sitting in Luigi's with the rest of my family, but I was sure he wouldn't mind if I let myself in and waited for him. I was just climbing into the taxi and giving the driver the address when a sudden, terrible thought struck me. Mum had obviously known what was going on. Had Grandad known, too? Pain swept through me again and I thought no, he couldn't have done. When I'd told him about Dad's ultimatum, he'd thought Kelly was over-dramatising things as usual. Until tonight, we'd both thought that Dave and my father had fallen out over dress codes.

My parents would be dropping Grandad home, but there wasn't much danger of them coming in; they wouldn't want a late night. I wondered what Kelly had told everyone about my abrupt disappearance. The truth? Or would she say I'd felt ill and had gone home? They might carry on and finish their meal. Dave wouldn't, I thought. Dave would come after me. Or at least the Dave I knew would have done.

The taxi pulled up outside Grandad's house and I paid the driver and walked round to the back garden. The sweetness of summer flowers hit me as I opened the gate. It was only just nine, but the nights were already drawing in. The moon was a silver dome and early stars were pinpricking the evening sky. As I found the key and let myself into the conservatory, I thought, with a little stab of pain, that the Dave I knew had disappeared for ever. The Dave I knew was the kind of man who'd bring me a cup of tea in bed every morning, the kind of man who'd work all hours to pay for an extravagant wedding present for my sister just to please me.

I sat in Grandad's rocking chair and moved the cane footstool so I could put my feet on it. I hoped he wouldn't mind finding me here. He'd often said the rocking motion helped him to think. It helped me to think, too. The more I rocked, the more I decided things didn't add up. If Dave really was seeing Kelly behind my back, surely he wouldn't be slogging his guts out to pay for her honeymoon with another man?

My mind was still churning when I heard Grandad's key in the front door just after ten. He came straight out to the conservatory, as I'd thought he would.

'Hi, Grandad,' I said quietly.

'Isobel? Princess, what are you doing sitting in the dark?' He stood silhouetted in the doorway and even the sight of him made me feel better. I got up at the same moment as he put the light on, blinking as my eyes adjusted.

'Come here, love.' He held out his arms and I went into them, feeling like a child again. He'd always been my rock. A thread of bright security in my life.

'Don't upset yourself,' he said. 'We'll get all this sorted out. Don't you worry.' As he stepped back a pace, he nearly fell over the cane footstool and it was my turn to hold on to him.

'I'll make us a cappuccino,' he said, when he'd recovered his balance. 'Or would you rather a brandy? I've got half a bottle in the cupboard.' He disappeared and came back a while later with a tray containing two cappuccinos, two mismatched tumblers and the brandy. He put the tray on the table, splashed brandy into the glasses and handed me one. 'It'll do you good,' he said, 'and I could certainly do with one.'

I sipped the pale gold liquid. 'Did Kelly tell you why I'd gone?'

He sighed. 'I sort of got the gist. Look, love, it's all a storm in a tea-cup, I'm sure. Like you said, arranging this wedding is getting to Kelly. She's wired up enough at the best of times.' He took a gulp of brandy. 'Don't worry. This'll all be sorted out by next weekend. It'll have to be.'

We looked at each other. I couldn't imagine going to Kelly's wedding now. I finished my brandy and decided it was helping. My churning thoughts were settling back into coherence. 'What did Dave do?'

'As soon as he realised what was going on, he went after you. He didn't even wait for his pizza. Mind you, things were getting a bit heated by then.'

'Why didn't he tell me, Grandad?' I said. I could hear the tremor in my voice. 'It was awful realising that everyone knew. All my family.'

'Not me, Princess. I'm as bowled down as you are. But it's Dave you should be talking to about this, not me.'

'I can't face him tonight. I don't suppose I could stay here, could I?'

''Course you can, but don't you think you ought to let him know where you are?'

'If I phone him now I'll end up saying something I regret. We both will.'

'Mmm, I've a feeling there's been enough of that tonight already.' He leaned across and poured me a second brandy. 'Medicinal purposes.'

'What would you do if you were me, Grandad?'

'Well, your gran would have said, 'Never let the sun go down on a row,' but sometimes maybe it's best to have a bit of a think through. I'd say you're doing the right thing, love. But then you always do. You've always been the sensible one, right from when you were a little girl.'

'Falling in love with Dave wasn't very sensible, was it?'

Tears rose in my voice and Grandad said gently, 'Love rarely is sensible, Princess, but the world would be a very dull place without it.' He leaned over and put his hand on the wooden arm of my chair, stilling its rocking for a moment. 'Love makes the world go round. You'll soon patch things up with that crazy sister of yours.'

'Do you think so?' A tear dripped into my brandy.

'I know so.' He yawned and pressed his fingers to his temples. 'The spare bed's made up. You get yourself a good night's rest. This will all look a lot better tomorrow. I promise.'

As I lay in the little single bed, with the rose-patterned wallpaper that hadn't changed since my childhood, I hoped that he was right. One thing was for sure. It couldn't get much worse.

★ ★ ★

The next day I awoke to the smell of frying bacon and when I wandered into the kitchen, I found Grandad standing at the cooker, a frying pan in his hand. 'How do you like your eggs?' he asked.

'You didn't have to cook me breakfast,' I told him.

'Well, as you didn't have any tea last night, I figured you'd be starving.' He looked at me over his glasses. 'Does this look done to you? I swear my eyesight gets worse every day.'

I smiled and decided not to tell him it was worse than he knew. The soap he'd put out for me in the bathroom was actually a round pink candle. I'd only noticed because it hadn't lathered and when I'd turned it over I'd discovered a little wick on the bottom.

'The bacon looks fine,' I said, realising he was right — I was hungry. 'Where are we having it?'

'I've laid the table in the greenhouse.' He waved a hand towards the conservatory. 'Nice in there this time of day. Gets the morning sun. And I can see what I'm eating.'

We sat among the plants, he in his rocking-chair now and me on an ordinary chair opposite. It wasn't until I'd demolished most of my breakfast that he said conversationally, 'Your Dave phoned up earlier.'

I put my fork down, my heart beginning to pound. 'What did he want?'

'Only to know if you were here. I said you were, but that you'd gone for a morning stroll and then you were coming home. I didn't want him racing round here before you were ready.'

'Thanks.'

'Don't mention it. Now, I'm not about to start giving you unwanted advice, but I do have a bit of a feeling. Here.' He put his hand over his chest.

'Wrong side,' I said wryly.

'Who said anything about where the feeling was?' He looked smug. 'That made you smile, didn't it? Anyway, this feeling I have — well, I don't think that Dave of yours is as big a villain as everyone else seems to think.'

'You don't?'

He buttered a slice of toast and handed it to me. 'You don't either, do you?'

'Well, no — but why did Kelly say it?'

'Heaven knows. You'll soon get to the top of things.'

'Bottom of things, you mean?'

'I've always thought the top is a better place to be than the bottom.' He winked. 'Now get that toast down you, get home and sort it out.'

I smiled at him. 'Thanks, Grandad.'

* * *

His warmth kept me going through the ten-minute walk back. I was sure by now that Grandad was right. There had to be an explanation and this morning I was calm enough to hear Dave's side of the story. But when I got close enough to see our drive, I could see that, although our car was back, Dave's works van had gone. There was a shaky feeling in the pit of my stomach as I let myself in the front door. So we weren't going to be able to sort this out straight away after all.

I walked through to the kitchen, which was as we'd left it. He obviously hadn't felt like breakfast. Upstairs, our bed didn't look as if it had been slept in. His baseball cap was still in the middle, where he'd left it the night before. I went and picked it up. Maybe he hadn't gone to work after all, but where else would he go on a Saturday morning? Surely nothing could be more important than sorting out things between us? I phoned his mobile, but the answerphone cut in. I left a message asking him to ring me.

I hadn't been back long when the doorbell chimed. The milkman, probably. We hadn't paid him for ages and last week he'd been reduced to leaving a sarcastic note but, what with everything that had been going on, I'd still forgotten. I grabbed my purse, an apology on my lips, but when I opened the door, it wasn't the milkman. It was Kelly.

'What do you want?'

'To talk to you.' She tossed her blonde hair and hugged her denim jacket around her. 'Can I come in? It's cold out here.'

'I've got nothing to say to you.'

'Please, Isobel.'

I was tempted to say no, but Grandad was right. I'd been the sensible one all our lives. Kelly was my sister and, however much she'd hurt me, I knew I was going to have to sort this out sooner or later. I opened the door and she stomped through to the kitchen.

She didn't sit down, just stood in the middle of the room, biting her lip. 'Are you still coming to the wedding?'

I could feel a little bubble of laughter rising in my throat. Only Kelly could ask such a question. 'What do you think?' I said, swallowing it down. 'Would you come to my wedding if I'd just told you I'd been having an affair with Tim?'

'Well no, but it's not the same thing, is it? I haven't been having an affair with Dave.'

'So you made it up, did you? Bit of a laugh, was it?' I couldn't stop the bitterness from creeping into my voice.

Kelly sighed. 'Don't you think you're overreacting? I mean, you didn't even know the guy then.'

I stared at her, not quite grasping the meaning of her words, and she sighed again.

'Izzy, look — it was years before you even met him.' She glanced at me, her expression changing from exasperation

44

to alarm. 'He did tell you that, didn't he?'

'I haven't seen him since last night,' I murmured, 'so no, he hasn't told me anything.'

'What do you mean you haven't seen him? Where is he, then?'

'Kelly, please just stop asking questions and explain, will you?'

'There's nothing much to explain. We met, we went on a few dates. We split up. End of story.'

'Hang on a minute. Are you saying that you went out with Dave before I did?'

She nodded, two little pink spots of colour on her cheekbones. 'Yes, that's what I was trying to tell you last night, but you flew off in a huff,' she said.

I shook my head. A strange mixture of relief and exasperation was rising inside me. So Grandad had been right. It had all been a storm in a tea-cup. 'But why the big secrecy? Why didn't you tell me when I introduced you that you already knew each other?'

'I wanted to, Izzy, truly I did, but Dave was adamant that I didn't. He said you had some massive paranoia about me stealing your boyfriends and it would only upset you.'

The paranoia accusation stung. Kelly had made a play for at least two of my boyfriends in the past, one of whom she'd ended up with. I decided to let it go for now and before I could say anything else the phone rang. I snatched it up. 'Dave?'

'No, it's me, Princess,' Grandad said. 'Sorry to bother you, but I thought I might try an optician after all. I wondered if you could do me a favour and book me an appointment.'

'Of course I can. Can't you find the number?'

'No.' He hesitated. 'I can't see it in the book. You know how my eyesight is.' He laughed, but there was something behind the laugh that worried me.

'Grandad, is something wrong?'

'No, not exactly. I've got a bit of a headache. Probably the brandy, eh?' He gave another little strained laugh. 'And everything's gone a bit blurry.'

'Blurry?'

'Yes, I'm sure it's nothing.'

'I'll come round,' I said, 'Kelly's here at the moment. We'll both come.' I put the phone down.

Kelly was already standing up. 'Is Grandad all right?'

'He says his eyes have gone blurry.'

'That sounds serious. What are you going to do?'

'Take him to casualty, I guess.'

'They'll refer him to the eye unit. That's where I went when I got that piece of grit in my eye. They'll know what to do.'

I didn't argue with her. Kelly's habit of making a drama out of every possible occasion extended to illnesses. She'd been in hospital more times than anyone else in our family — usually not for long, once they found out there was very little wrong with her.

In the car, I said, 'So come on, then.

What's going on between Dad and Dave?'

She sighed theatrically. 'Do you remember when I was taking my driving lessons and I borrowed Dad's car for a session when they were away on holiday?'

'Yes, vaguely,' I said distractedly. Half my mind was on Grandad. He was never ill. He never even went to the doctor's.

'And I had a bit of a near-miss with the gatepost?' Kelly went on.

'It wasn't a near-miss, you wrote off the front wing.'

'Yes, well, whatever,' Kelly replied. 'Do you remember?'

I nodded. 'That car was his pride and joy. He went on about it for months.'

'Exactly,' Kelly said. 'He was furious. He threatened to chuck me out so . . . Well, I told him it wasn't my fault. I said I hadn't been driving.'

'What's that got to do with anything?'

'I told Dad that the boyfriend who was giving me lessons was driving and he'd done a runner without giving me his address. I mean, I still had to pay for the damage because the insurance wouldn't cough up, but it got me off the hook with Dad.'

'I'm not with you,' I said, indicating to turn right into the tree-lined road where Grandad lived.

'Well, Dad's just found out that the boyfriend concerned was your Dave,' she said.

'He's what?' I stalled the car in the middle of the road and stared at her in amazement.

She stared back indignantly. 'It seemed like a good idea at the time. I still had to pay for the thing and I'd finished with Dave by the time our parents came back from holiday, so he didn't know anything about it. Look, Izzy, it worked, didn't it? I didn't get kicked out. The Jag got paid for — well almost. And Dave didn't get into trouble because Dad never even met him. How was I to know you'd end up going out with him?'

'But how did Dad find out about all this now?'

'Ah, well . . . ' She sounded nervous. 'Well, actually, Tim told him. The bloke behind us is flashing his lights,' she added casually. 'I think we're in his way.'

I restarted the car, pulled up outside Grandad's house and turned towards her. 'So, how did Tim know about it? Did you tell him?'

'No, of course I didn't tell him. He didn't even know I'd been out with Dave until the other night. We were out with some friends and one of them said wasn't it a coincidence that you and I had both been out with the same bloke? We had a bit of a row about it, actually.'

'Why did you tell Tim about the car?'

'I didn't,' she replied. 'He and Dad went out for a male bonding session and Dave's name came up. Dad worked out the timing and put two and two together. Tim didn't know about the car until Dad threw a wobbler.'

'So let me get this straight,' I said.

'Dad thinks Dave wrecked his pride and joy, then disappeared into the sunset without so much as an apology?'

'Er, yes. That about sums it up.' She got out of the car before I could say anything else.

I caught up with her at the gate. 'But it was *you* who hit that gatepost. You only blamed someone else to get you off the hook!'

'Stop shouting at me, Izzy.'

'You're going to have to sort it out. Put the record straight and tell Dad that Dave had nothing to do with it.' I grabbed hold of her arm.

She shrugged me off. 'I can't,' she answered. 'At least not till after the wedding. He'll go mad at me for lying to him and he's paying for most of it.'

'I don't believe you sometimes.' I let us into the back garden and Kelly hurried ahead of me.

Grandad was sitting in his rocking-chair, with the *Yellow Pages* open on his lap. As I opened the conservatory door, he looked up. 'You didn't need to come, love. I'll be fine just as soon as these painkillers kick in.'

He looked white. I went across and knelt by his chair. 'How long have you had the pain? Why didn't you mention it earlier?'

'Well, it wasn't too bad then, but it's got worse. I can't find my glasses.' He broke off and grinned at me, only he wasn't looking quite in my direction and I realised that he couldn't see me at all.

'Grandad, how many fingers am I holding up?'

'Five.'

'Very good.' A little chill of shock crept through me. I hadn't been holding up any fingers. Grandad couldn't see me at all.

'I think we'll take you to the hospital. Just to check things out.'

'Hospital?'

'Just as a precaution. Come on.'

'Izzy's right, Grandad,' Kelly said. 'Eyes are too important to mess about with.'

Grandad jumped and I realised with a jolt that he hadn't even known my sister was in the room.

We went out the back way, Grandad walking between us, remarkably steadily for someone who couldn't see. It struck me that his eyesight must have been failing for ages, but he probably hadn't known the extent of it himself. He'd just adjusted, as his days got darker and darker.

On the way to the hospital, Kelly kept up a stream of bright chatter about the wedding arrangements and Grandad responded equally brightly. Even though I was still furious with my sister, I could appreciate what she was doing. Odd, I thought, that when there really was a drama, Kelly was a good person to have around.

Within minutes of booking Grandad into the accident and emergency unit, he was whisked off into a cubicle.

'God, it must be pretty serious for them to see him that quickly,' Kelly said, sitting on the plastic chair beside me and resting her chin in her hands.

'I'll wait with him if you want to go off and sort out your wedding bits and pieces,' I offered.

'No, it's all right. I'll stay.' She touched my arm. 'I'm worried about him too, you know,' she said quietly. 'Look, I really am sorry about Dave and the car and stuff. It's just an unfortunate sequence of events.'

'Well, we're going to have to sort it out before Saturday,' I told her firmly. 'We're going to have to speak to Dad.'

'Yes, I suppose we are.' She screwed up her face. 'God, I've got a headache. Hey, you don't suppose I've got anything wrong with *my* eyes, do you? Maybe I ought to have them checked while we're here.'

The nurse reappeared from the cubicle. 'Isobel and Kelly?' she asked. 'Mr Simmonds' granddaughters?'

We stood up in unison.

'We've done an eyesight test and now I'm going to take him down to see the specialist. He wanted me to let you know.' She smiled. 'Don't look so worried, we'll soon have him sorted out.'

Kelly glanced at her watch. 'How long will he be?'

'About half an hour, I should think.'

'I need to make a couple of phone calls,' Kelly said. 'Can I borrow your mobile, Izzy?'

'You'll have to use that outside,' the nurse told her.

Kelly nodded and disappeared through the double doors. I ought to try Dave again, although it was just as well I'd spoken to Kelly first. If I'd have gone home last night, bitter with jealousy, God knows what I'd have said to him.

I was just getting up to follow Kelly outside when she hurriedly came back in.

'Izzy, Mum just phoned. Apparently Dave turned up about half an hour ago and insisted on speaking to Dad.'

'Dave's at our parents'?'

She nodded. 'Mum wanted us to go straight round.'

'Did you tell her where we were?'

'Yes, but I think we're going to have to go, Izzy. Or at least you are. It doesn't sound like it's going too well. Mum said they're on the verge of having a punch-up.'

3

My head was spinning as I drove to my parents' house. 'Are you sure Mum said they were about to have a punch-up?' I'd asked Kelly, out of Grandad's hearing, just before I left. He had enough on his plate without more worry.

'She said Dad was shouting his head off.' She'd looked worried. 'I'm so sorry, Izzy. I should have told him first.'

I'd tried to phone Mum back, but the answerphone was on, so in the end I'd left Kelly sitting with Grandad at the hospital, still waiting to see the specialist.

I'd know soon enough what was going on anyway. My parents lived about fifteen minutes from the hospital. I was almost there when my mobile rang. It was tucked in my handbag, in the footwell by the passenger seat. I slowed the car down a bit. I could just about reach it if I bent down and leaned across.

At the same moment that my fingers made contact with the phone, the car in front of me braked sharply. Instinct slammed my foot on to the brake pedal. There was a bang, followed by a searing pain in my face. Then a brief, hazy darkness. The next thing I was aware of was that I was leaning forward on the steering wheel and there was blood dripping on to my lap. Blood dripping on to my favourite jeans, I remember thinking. It would be hell getting it out of the fabric seats of the car.

'Are you all right? I say, are you all right?'

The voice could have been coming from anywhere, but finally I located it as coming from somewhere over to my right. A draft of air was coming from the same direction. The driver's door was open. Someone must have opened it I turned my head, with difficulty.

'My God. Just hold on there.

Ambulance is on its way.'

As soon as his face came into focus, I wished it hadn't. Judging by his horrified expression, I must look a mess.

'Don't you worry, now.' He crouched down next to me and I was aware of cream chinos close to my face. You'd never get the blood out of those. I put my hand out to push him away and, misinterpreting my gesture he grabbed hold of it.

'It's OK I'll stay with you till they get here.'

'I'm fine,' I said, but it came out as, 'I'm thine.' The blood, I decided, was coming mainly from my nose, which I must have bashed on the steering wheel. There was a sore patch on my face and my head hurt like hell.

I groaned and he squeezed my hand. 'Won't be long now.'

After that things were a bit of a blur. Blue lights, reassuring voices and a rather tasty-looking paramedic. Why did you never see them when you were looking your best?

'I don't need to go to hospital.'

'Just a precaution, love. You've hit your head. Do you remember if you lost consciousness at all?'

One of the paramedics picked up my mobile phone and shook his head. 'These things ought to be banned from cars.'

Oh great, so I was going to be done for dangerous driving as well. And by now, Dave and Dad were probably killing each other. At this rate, my whole family could end up at the same hospital. I began to laugh, but it came out as a sob. At least they'd managed to stop the bleeding, but it was too late for my jeans.

Just as I was being helped into the ambulance, I looked around for Mr White Chinos, but he was talking to a policeman. I wondered if I'd done much damage to his car. And ours, come to that.

I'd never been in an ambulance before. It was smaller than I'd expected. There was a kind of bench seat, lots of equipment and what looked like someone's sandwich wrapper from lunch on the floor. My face throbbed and I closed my eyes. This was the sort of thing that happened to Kelly, not me.

The ambulance drew up at the opposite end of the hospital to where I'd left her and Grandad about half an hour ago, and I was taken into a small, curtained cubicle.

'It's a lot better than it looks,' the nurse said, smiling, when she'd finished cleaning me up. 'You've got a little cut above your lip that will need a couple of stitches and you're going to have a lovely black eye for a few days.'

'My nose feels broken.'

'It's not, just a bit bashed around.'

'I'm going to my sister's wedding next Saturday. Am I going to ruin all the photos?'

She frowned and I could see she was trying to think of something diplomatic to say.

Maybe it wouldn't matter anyway, I

thought. Dave and Dad may well have had an irretrievable breakdown of communication by now, and Grandad was in hospital too. At this rate there wouldn't be any close family there. Poor Kelly. Then I reminded myself that none of this would have happened if she hadn't lied to Dad about Dave. Except for Grandad's eyes, of course. I couldn't blame her for that. I wondered how he was getting on.

'It's amazing what you can do with the right make-up,' the nurse said eventually.

I nodded. 'Actually, my sister's wedding is the least of my worries,' I told her. 'My grandad's in the eye unit at the moment. Is there any chance of getting a message to him?'

'He's here?'

'Yes.'

'I'll just get someone to put these stitches in and you can go down there yourself.'

'I don't have to stay in overnight or anything?'

'Well, we'll see what the doctor says, but I shouldn't think so.'

She was right, as it turned out. Once the doctor had confirmed there was someone to look after me at home, he said I could go. The first thing I did was to nip into the loos and look in the mirror. I would have burst into tears, except that too much movement hurt my face. No wonder the nurse had been cagey about whether I'd look all right for Kelly's wedding. I'd seen opponents of Mike Tyson's looking more attractive.

In medical terms, the doctor had probably done a neat job of the cut above my lip, but right now it looked as though a spiky caterpillar was stuck to my face. There was a purplish bruise below one eye and my cheekbone was sore. By the day of Kelly's wedding, my face would be a multi-coloured patchwork mess. The right make-up was the understatement of the year. I'd need a bag over my head at the very least. I turned away from the mirror.

On the plus side, I thought ruefully, my jeans weren't as bad as I thought. Aware that I'd have to get a taxi back, I sponged them with a paper towel and finished them off under the dryer. Then I walked down to the eye unit.

There was no sign of Grandad or Kelly in the waiting room. I looked at my watch. A quarter past two, although it felt much later. Perhaps they'd got a taxi back to Grandad's. I went outside the hospital to phone them, but I couldn't get my mobile to work. I could have gone back inside and used the call box, but I'd had enough of hospitals for one day. I screwed up my face in frustration, and immediately regretted it. Now what should I do? Go straight home, or to my parents, or Grandad's?

Indecision hovered over me. I still hadn't made up my mind when I got into one of the taxis outside the main entrance of the hospital.

'Where to, love?' asked the driver, not batting an eyelid at the state of my face.

I realised he had the same bushy

eyebrows as Grandad, and, before I'd thought about it, I'd given him Grandad's address. Then I rested my head back on the seat and closed my eyes.

★　★　★

'My God, what on earth happened to you?' Kelly's face was a picture as she opened Grandad's front door.

'It's a long story.'

'Well, I think you'd better tell me. Was it Dad or was it Dave?'

'What?'

'Who thumped you? Honestly, Izzy, I never thought they'd turn on you. This is getting worse and worse. I just can't believe this is happening.'

'Kelly, no one's thumped me. I had an accident.'

'An accident?' She looked as though she was going to burst into tears. 'What sort of an accident?'

'Just a little shunt with another car. Nothing serious.'

'But your face is a complete mess.'

'Thanks very much. Yes, I had spotted that. According to the nurse, it's not as bad as it looks.'

'Is that you, Isobel?' Grandad's voice carried along the hallway. 'What's all the shouting?'

'Yes, it's me. Just coming. How is he?' I asked Kelly, who was still staring at my face with thinly disguised horror. 'What did they say about his eyes?'

'He's got some kind of auto-immune disorder,' she told me. 'To do with inflammation of the iris or something. He's got a leaflet that tells you all about it.'

'It is curable, though? I mean, is he going to be able to see normally once they've sorted it out?'

'Hopefully, if he hasn't done too much damage by ignoring it. He's got a load of eye drops to use. That's why I came back with him. Just to make sure he knows which bottle is which.' She hesitated and whispered, rather belatedly I thought, 'He can't see a thing at

66

the moment, but that's just as well, the state you're in.'

Grandad was in his chair in the conservatory. 'Is that you, Princess?'

'Yes, it's me.' I knelt beside his chair and put my hand over his. 'How are you feeling? Headache gone now?'

'I'm all right.' He grinned. 'Lot of fuss about nothing if you ask me. Just some silly infection or something.'

'It's not an infection, it's an inflammation,' Kelly corrected, coming into the conservatory. 'You must do exactly as the doctor said, Grandad. Eye drops every hour.' Her voice was all stern and fierce and I smiled at her.

Grandad screwed up his face and said in a stage whisper, 'Bossy madam, your sister, isn't she?'

'She's right, though,' I told him. 'Your eyes are too precious to mess around with.'

'The world looks perfectly fine to me,' he said, squinting at me, but he didn't mention my face. I thought again that Grandad didn't see the same world as the rest of us anyway. He saw a world of his own making — had done for maybe a lot longer than any of us realised.

'Time for your eye drops,' Kelly said. 'Now listen, I've put an elastic band round the four-hour one, so you know which one's which. And I've set the timer on your watch so you know when to take them.'

'I'm not completely helpless,' Grandad protested.

'You can phone Izzy's mobile if you get stuck,' my sister went on. 'It's the third button down on your phone.'

'Yes, yes.' Grandad muttered. 'Don't go on.'

I watched her fussing around him and reflected that she was actually being very sensible. If she hadn't been so prone to histrionics, she'd have made a good nurse.

We left Grandad's at about three and walked back to my house to get Kelly's car.

'What do you think Dave's told

Dad?' she asked, as we drew in sight of my driveway and could see that his van was back.

'I don't know.' My face was starting to throb. All I really wanted to do now was to lie down in a nice dark room with no mirrors in it.

'Should I come in and apologise?'

'No, let me talk to him first. You go and sort out your bits and pieces.'

She looked relieved. 'I'll pop in and see Dad on the way back. I might as well get it over with.'

I nodded, then waited until she'd driven off and let myself into the house.

Dave was in the kitchen, sitting at the table, reading a paper. As I came into the room, he glanced up, did a double-take and jumped out of his chair. 'Good grief, Isobel, what's happened?'

'You should see the other guy.'

'Don't mess about. What on earth have you been doing? I've been trying to phone you.' Stress lines wrinkled his forehead and his eyes were dark with worry. He came across the kitchen and put out a tentative finger to my face.

'Careful, it's sore.'

'It looks it.'

'I need to lie down,' I told him. 'I'll go in the lounge. Any chance of some painkillers?'

It was nice in our lounge, cool and peaceful and out of sight of the world. I sank on to our ancient, squashy sofa and rested my head against a cushion. With a bit of luck, I'd nod off and when I woke up none of this would have happened. It'd still be yesterday, before we'd gone to Luigi's, before Grandad's eyes had packed up, before Kelly had told me she'd been out with Dave before I had.

Dave came hurrying in with my painkillers and a glass of water. He knelt by the sofa. 'I thought I'd had a bad day,' he said, with a wry smile, 'but yours looks like it's been worse, so you'd better start.'

I tried not to smile back. Movement pulled the stitches on my face. I swallowed the tablets and filled him in on what had happened since last night, or at least an abridged version that included Grandad's eyesight problems and the car shunt. I didn't mention the bitter jealousy that had swept through me when Kelly had told me they'd had a fling. Last night seemed a long time ago now.

'I was worried sick when you didn't come home,' he said, studying my face.

'Sorry. I was upset.'

'I came after you, but you'd vanished. It didn't occur to me until this morning that you might be at your grandad's. Then when I phoned and he said you'd gone for a walk. Well, I just couldn't wait any longer. I thought the best thing I could do was to go and thrash it out with your father once and for all.'

'And have you?'

'Well, when I first turned up, he was all right. Showed me into the dining room, told your mum not to disturb us. Then, once he'd lulled me into a false sense of security, he just let rip. Shouted at me for about five minutes. I couldn't get a word in edgeways. It took me a while to realise what he was so angry about. Then it dawned on me that Kelly had told him it was me who'd pranged his car.'

'Did you put him straight?'

He paused. 'Not exactly, no. I was so taken aback, I didn't say a lot, to be honest. He wouldn't have listened anyway. He was too busy shouting.'

'So he still thinks it was you?'

'Kelly ought to be the one to tell him, oughtn't she?'

'She should be doing that about now,' I said, and hoped that she was. 'Dave, why didn't you tell me you already knew her when I first introduced you?'

He hesitated, looking away from me, his face in profile. 'I suppose because I knew how things were between you — that you were sensitive about her pinching your boyfriends. You'd mentioned it often enough. I was afraid that

if I told you, you'd feel second-best —
no matter how long ago it had been or
how little it meant.' His voice was quiet.
'I wasn't trying to deceive you, Isobel. I
didn't know she was your sister until
that night.'

I looked into his brown eyes, which
were more serious than I'd ever seen
them. And I believed him.

'Hey, you didn't think I'd really had
an affair with her when I was with you?'

'No,' I said wearily. It seemed a long
time since Kelly's revelations. A lifetime
ago that I'd run out of Luigi's and into
the rain. 'It was just a bit of a shock,
that's all.'

'I'm sorry.' He reached for my hand.
'I should have told you ages ago. I was
just so paranoid that I might lose you.'

I looked at him, surprised. Dave
never said anything serious about
emotions. It wasn't his style.

Before either of us could say anything
else, the phone rang. Dave went across
and picked it up. 'Your mum,' he said,
handing it to me on the settee.

'Isobel, Kelly's just told us you had a bump. 'Are you all right? She said you had stitches in your face.'

'I'm OK.'

There was an awkward pause and then she went on. 'Kelly's also told us the truth about what happened.'

'With Dad's car?'

'Yes, love. I can't tell you how sorry I am. Poor Dave. Your father gave him a right earful this afternoon. He's coming over later to apologise.'

'Blimey,' I said. 'That'll be a first.'

'Your father might be a bit stubborn,' Mum said primly, 'but he always does the right thing in the end.'

Later that night, Dave and Dad sat in our back room, each with a can of lager, although Dad's was alcohol-free. When I went in, they were getting on like a house on fire.

Mum sat next to Dad on the settee with a glass of sherry in her hand. 'Your sister might be a pain in the neck, but at least she's put everything right now,' she said, smiling.

I decided it would be uncharitable to point out that my face felt far from all right and just nodded.

'Nothing else can go wrong,' Mum said.

I wished I shared her confidence. We still had a week to go. Anything could happen.

* * *

On Wednesday night, I had a frantic phone call from Kelly saying that the DJ had a bad case of food poisoning and wasn't sure if he was going to be able to make it. Then, on Thursday, the caterers rang Dad to say they'd only had two bottles of bubbly delivered for the toast and was that right? Luckily Mum overheard him saying that it sounded fine to him as it would save anyone getting drunk, and confirmed that the original order was two crates.

By Friday afternoon, I was beginning to feel quietly optimistic. The DJ said he was feeling better, but his brother had agreed to step in if he couldn't make it. Kelly had got me a whole stack of potions and lotions from the chemist that promised to reduce my bruising. Our pharmacist had been brilliant. When Kelly had explained about the wedding, she'd recommended a make-up artist who specialised in disguising scars.

We'd been to see her and she'd looked at the damage and said, 'The stitches might be a bit tricky, but the rest is no problem. I can make up your face for you, if you like? On the day, I mean.'

We'd accepted her offer gratefully.

Kelly, meanwhile, had been subdued all week. She couldn't stop apologising to Dave.

'I know it was nothing personal,' he said, his mouth twisting into a wry smile. 'It just got you out of a tricky situation.'

'It made it worse in the long run.' Kelly sounded genuinely contrite.

'Don't worry about it. I'm not.'

'He's really nice, isn't he?' she said to

me later. 'I mean, there's a lot more to him than meets the eye.'

I smiled at her. 'I guess there is to most people, if you think about it. Dad's been really nice too, hasn't he?'

'Yes, thank God.' She frowned. 'Tim's more of a dark horse than I thought, though. We had a bit of a row last night, actually.'

'Last-minute wedding nerves?'

'I hope so. He told me that he'd nearly got married once before, but he chickened out at the last minute.'

I looked at her in alarm. 'What do you mean?'

'What I mean,' Kelly said softly, 'is that he left her standing at the altar. He's never mentioned it before. He's never even told me he was engaged. You don't think he was trying to . . . well, say something, do you?'

'Like what?'

'Like he was having second thoughts.'

'Did he say he was?'

'Well, no, but I'm worried.' She looked as if she'd like to say something else, then thought better of it.

'I'm sure he wouldn't have mentioned it at all if he was planning a repeat performance.'

'No, I expect you're right,' Kelly said, but she didn't look convinced.

I'd taken the week off to help Kelly with last-minute stuff and by Thursday night we were ready. Hire-cars, the first-night reservation and the reception venue, which were at the same hotel, were all confirmed. The three-tier wedding cake had been collected and dropped off at the hotel. In the interests of tradition, Kelly was staying with us the night before the wedding. Her dress was in our spare room, along with my outfit. Creamy satin and simply cut, it was beautiful.

Just before bedtime, I went in to look at it and wondered if Dave and I would ever get married. It seemed unlikely. Marriage, Dave had said earlier in the week, was for traditionalists. A lot of expense and fuss, designed for romantics.

'And we're not romantics?' I'd said, half-wistful.

'I'm too cynical to be a romantic.' He'd smiled. 'And you're too sensible, I'd say.'

'So sensible that I wrecked our car and ruined my looks a week before my sister's big day.'

'Extenuating circumstances,' Dave said.

Now, he came into the room behind me. 'What are you doing?'

'Just admiring Kelly's dress. Beautiful, isn't it?'

'It's all right, I suppose.' He yawned. 'Come to bed. It's late.'

★ ★ ★

On the Saturday, I'd arranged to pick up Grandad early so he could get ready for the wedding at our place.

'How are your eyes?' I said, as he collected up his bottles of eye drops and painkillers.

'Good as new,' he said, tripping over

79

his bag, which I'd put ready by the front door. 'How's your sister?'

'Nervous.'

'Yes, well that's understandable. And you?' He peered at me. 'What on earth have you done to your face?'

'Nothing that a good make-up artist can't put right, apparently,' I told him.

'Beauty is on the inside, not the outside,' he murmured.

'You always say the right thing, don't you?' I replied, feeling unexpected tears spring to my eyes.

'Yes, well, that's because I'm a very clear thinker,' he said smugly. 'So how's the weather forecast? No chance of it cracking up before the wedding?'

'It's a beautiful day,' I told him. 'Not a cloud in the sky. A perfect day for a wedding.'

We got back to our house just as the flowers were being delivered. I carried them in and put them on the kitchen table. Dave was on his mobile in the hall.

'Everything OK?' I mouthed, as he disconnected.

'Er, not sure.' He glanced up the stairs and lowered his voice. 'That was Paul, Tim's best man. Apparently he was taking him for a pre-wedding breakfast this morning, but he can't get any answer.'

'Maybe he's overslept or something. It's only half-past eight.'

'That's what I said, but Paul didn't seem to think so. He said the car's not there either.'

'Are the flowers here yet?' Kelly shouted from the top of the stairs.

'Yes, they've just arrived.' I called.

'What's the matter? You look worried.'

Dave, who had his back to her, raised his eyebrows helplessly.

'Everything's fine, sweetheart,' Grandad called up the stairs. 'I'm just coming up to give you a hand.'

Kelly grinned. 'God, I'm nervous. Nothing else is going to go wrong, is it?'

'Course it isn't,' Grandad soothed.

He turned back towards us and said under his breath, 'I'll sort Kelly out. You go and track down the groom.'

'Fine,' I said, but my stomach was tying itself into knots. I didn't know Tim very well, and neither did Dave. As for tracking him down, I didn't have a clue where to start.

4

Dave grabbed my hand and pulled me into the kitchen. 'It's probably best if you stay here with Kelly,' he said. 'If we both go out, she'll suspect something's wrong. I said I'd phone Paul back on my mobile outside in case Kelly comes down. He knows most of Tim's mates. We'll find him, don't worry.'

I squeezed his hand. 'Good luck.'

'It'll be fine.' He disappeared out of the back door and I hoped he was right. I looked at the flowers spread out on the table. The kitchen was full of their sweet scent; Kelly's bouquet of pink and white carnations, pink roses, and lacy ferns, so delicate they didn't look real. I went across and picked up my own bouquet, a mini version of Kelly's. Closing my eyes, I held it to my face, the blooms cool on my cheek. This morning was beginning to take on an unreal quality too, or had that happened earlier when everything started to spiral out of control? Perhaps when I'd rushed out of Luigi's, when Kelly had told me she'd had a fling with Dave. Or the next day, when I'd nosedived the steering wheel and ended up in the same hospital as Grandad. Maybe I'd bashed my head harder than I'd thought. Perhaps this was all some kind of crazy hallucination. Normal families didn't have weddings like this, surely. Things went wrong, yes, but not on this scale. This wedding had tipped our family upside down.

Kelly had said as much last night, when she'd dragged me into our bathroom where she'd been painting her toenails, and asked if I'd mind finishing them off because her hands were shaking too much. She'd perched on the edge of the bath and I'd sat on the fluffy loo seat, with her feet balanced on my lap.

'Perhaps it's because it's not meant

to be,' she'd said. 'Perhaps it's because I'm a bad person, Isobel, and I don't deserve to be happy.'

'You're not a bad person, don't be silly.' I'd glanced at her between brush strokes. She wasn't given to fits of insecurity, my sister. Flights of fantasy, maybe, but never self-doubt.

'What goes around, comes around,' Kelly said quietly. 'If I hadn't told Dad that Dave had crashed his car then none of this would be happening.'

'Don't be ridiculous. It's not your fault the DJ got food poisoning or the caterers messed up the order. It's not your fault Grandad's eyes started playing him up.' I'd looked at her beautiful face and added, 'Anyway, everything's sorted now and Dad and Dave are getting on fine. You've just got last-minute nerves, that's all. All brides have them.'

'Do you think so?' She looked like a little girl and I felt a rush of compassion.

'Nothing else is going to go wrong,' I

told her. 'Just relax and look forward to your big day.'

Why had I said that? I thought now, my stomach knotting. What if Dave and Paul couldn't find Tim? Everything else that had gone wrong was irrelevant in comparison. The doorbell interrupted my thoughts. It was the hairdresser.

'All set?' She beamed at me. 'Everything under control?'

'We're getting there.' I ushered her upstairs and glanced at my watch. Kelly was getting married at twelve-thirty. We had just under three hours.

Grandad came down while the hairdresser was at work and we sat in the kitchen and discussed things. 'What if they can't find Tim? We're going to have to tell her. We can't let her turn up if he doesn't.'

'He'll be there.' Grandad put his hand over mine. 'I'm a good judge of character. Tim's just got a touch of the collywobbles. I was the same when I married your grandmother.'

Kelly couldn't have told him that her

intended had already left one bride standing at the altar, I thought. Perhaps he was a serial jilter.

At eleven o'clock, I phoned Dave on his mobile. 'What's happening?'

'No sign of him, love. Paul thinks we ought to say something. He says he had a feeling Tim might do something like this. He was edgy last night when he spoke to him.'

'Then why didn't he warn us? We might have been able to sort things out.'

'I doubt it would have made any difference. If Tim doesn't want to get married, there isn't a lot we could have done about it, is there?'

'At least we could have stopped it getting this far. It'll break Kelly's heart if he backs out now.'

'We'll have to tell her, love. Look, we'll be back in about ten minutes. If you want to hold fire until we get there, then fine. But we've got to say something soon.'

I put the phone down and told

Grandad what was happening. Then the doorbell rang and the make-up artist and Mum and Dad arrived at the same time.

I let everyone in. Mum, looking beautiful in her lilac dress and new hat, and Dad stiff and smart in his hired suit. Dave was right, I thought. We couldn't let this go on any longer. I asked the make-up artist to wait in the lounge. After all, it didn't look as if we were going to require her services now. Then I hustled Mum and Dad into the kitchen and told them what was happening.

'I'll throttle Tim,' my father said and Mum looked as if she was going to cry.

'Just wait five more minutes,' Grandad said.

'The hairdresser's ready to do your hair, Isobel,' Kelly called from the top of the stairs. 'Is the make-up lady here yet?'

The phone rang again before anyone could answer her.

'Have you said anything to Kelly yet?' Dave hissed.

'No.'

'Well, don't, we've found him. We called back to his house on the off chance and he was there.'

'So is he having second thoughts, or what?'

'I'm not sure. Paul's having a chat with him right now.'

'They're supposed to be getting married in an hour. Is it on or is it off? I need to know.'

'I'll phone you back in five minutes.'

I relayed the news to everyone in the kitchen and a collective sigh of relief went round.

'There may still be a problem,' I said. 'He's phoning back.'

'Isobel,' Kelly shouted, 'are you coming to get ready?'

'Two seconds,' I called, at the same moment as the phone rang again.

'I'll get that.' My father strode across the kitchen. We all waited while he listened, his face expressionless. 'What do you intend to do about it?' he said at last. 'Apologising's no good, is it? We're all waiting to go to a wedding.'

I could feel my heart sinking. Looked like Tim had cried off after all. Poor, poor Kelly. I watched as my father slammed the phone down. 'This is beyond a joke,' he said, looking round at us all. 'That was the car hire company. Seems they've had a shunt on the motorway and put the car out of action. They won't be able to take us.'

I closed my eyes, a mixture of relief and panic flooding through me.

'I should think that's the least of our problems,' Grandad said. 'We can get a taxi if we have to.'

'My daughter's not going to her wedding in a taxi,' Dad said, bristling.

'Look, Peter, she might not be going at all, if the groom doesn't turn up.' That was Mum. I left them still talking heatedly and went to find Kelly.

'What's going on down there? It sounds pretty hectic. Is Mum coming up?'

'Stop wriggling about,' the make-up

artist bossed. 'Or you'll have lipstick in your ear.'

'Everything's fine,' I lied and escaped to the bathroom to wash my hair. Kelly sat on the bed, firing questions at me, as the hairdresser styled it. 'Everything's going to be all right, isn't it, Izzy?'

'Course it is.'

She was still wrapped in her dressing-gown. The dress hung on the picture rail behind her, its skirt smoothed out on the bed to stop the creases. It gleamed softly in the sunlight coming through the net curtains.

'When are you putting it on?' I said, standing up to admire my finished hair.

'Not until the last minute. I don't want to tempt fate.'

'You can talk while I'm doing your face,' said the make-up artist, patting the chair by the dressing-table mirror. 'Come and sit down again. Time's getting on.'

In the mirror I watched her expertly covering my bruises with concealer and wondered what was happening down-stairs.

'All done,' she said, with satisfaction. 'Can't do much about your cut lip, but it'll hardly notice in the photographs.' She stood up, smiling.

'Thank you,' I murmured, meeting Kelly's gaze in the mirror. No one had come rushing up to tell Kelly that it was all off, so I figured that Tim had got over his last minute doubts.

'You're quiet,' Kelly said. 'What are you thinking?'

'Nothing much. I'll just nip down and make sure everything's OK.'

'Put your dress on first. There's something I want to tell you.'

I was about to object, but her eyes were insistent so, as soon as we were alone again, I pulled the rose pink dress over my head.

'Turn round, I'll button it. You look beautiful,' Kelly said.

'What did you want to tell me?' It had been quiet downstairs for a while and I was beginning to get edgy.

'Only that you're going to be an auntie. I'm pregnant, Izzy. Are you pleased?'

I blinked, my eyes going automatically to her stomach.

'Oh, it doesn't show yet.' She flattened the robe so I could see. 'I'm only a very little bit pregnant.'

'Does Tim know?'

'No, he doesn't, actually.' She smiled. 'I only found out myself last night for sure and I didn't have time to tell him. I did a test just before I came round and he was just dashing up to the shops.'

A sudden, vivid image of Kelly's untidy flat flew into my mind. She never put anything away. It would be typical of her to leave the tester kit in full view on the sink or the bathroom cabinet. It wouldn't occur to her that Tim might see it and cotton on. Was that why he'd disappeared? If he'd been edgy about marriage, what would the added responsibility of a baby do to him?

'What's the matter, Izzy? Aren't you pleased?'

'Yes, of course. I've always wanted to be an auntie.' The words came automatically, but I realised, with a small start of surprise, that they were true. 'Kelly, do you think Tim will be pleased? I mean, when are you going to tell him?'

'I'll tell him later on. He'll be thrilled. He's always wanted kids.'

Wanting kids and finding out one was on the way the night before your wedding were two different things, I thought, but I didn't contradict her. She looked so happy.

'I know we haven't always seen eye to eye, Izzy, and it's mostly my fault because I'm a selfish bag, but I do love you. That's why I wanted you to be the first to know.' She hugged her arms around herself. 'Auntie Izzy — it's got a certain ring to it, hasn't it?'

'Yes,' I said. 'I'll just nip downstairs and check everything's on schedule, then I'll come and give you a hand with your dress.'

'You won't tell Mum, will you?'

I shook my head. 'Course I won't.' I went across and hugged her. 'I love you, too, you know.'

Downstairs, I found Mum sitting on her own in the kitchen, looking tense.

'Is everything OK? Where's Dad?'

'He's gone with Dave to pick up the Jaguar. Dave's going to drive him and your sister to church.'

'Dad's letting Dave drive his new car?'

'He suggested it. Well, it's that or a taxi. He had a right barney with the car hire firm, but they can't produce a car out of nothing. Even your father had to accept it in the end.'

'So where's Tim? Was he having last-minute doubts?'

She frowned. 'Paul's not sure. He said not. He's obviously got something on his mind, but he refused point blank to discuss it. Then your grandad insisted on going out for a chat. They're in the garden now.'

'I'd assumed Grandad was getting ready?'

'He said there's no point until he's made sure Tim's definitely serious.'

'About the wedding?'

'About the marriage,' Mum said quietly. 'Your grandad said it's no good Dave and Paul bullying him into going through with it. He's gone to make sure he really wants to marry Kelly. I tried to talk him out of it, but he was adamant, Isobel.' She stood up. 'He's right, you know. It's not just about today, is it? It's about the rest of their lives. Tim has to be sure this is what he really wants. Ironic, isn't it,' she added, 'that Grandad sees everything so clearly? Despite being the only one of us who can't see much at all.'

I stood looking at her, taking all this in. 'Shall I go and see how they're getting on?'

'I should leave them to it, love.'

'But we're going to be leaving in a few minutes.'

'Mum, are you there?' Kelly's voice came from the top of the stairs. 'Is anybody there? I need a hand with my dress. I'm supposed to be getting married in half an hour.'

'If anything else goes wrong, come and get me,' Mum whispered and disappeared.

I stood in the empty kitchen. Guests would be arriving at the church about now. A strange calm descended on me, perhaps because everything was in the hands of the gods. I wondered what Grandad was saying to Tim and hoped he wouldn't make things any worse.

And that's when I heard the crash from the back garden. Gathering up my dress to stop it dragging on the ground, I charged outside and found Grandad sitting in our newly-planted rosemary bush.

'What on earth are you doing?'

'I didn't see the fork.' He kicked the offending item in an uncharacteristic show of bad temper. 'I think I've broken my finger.'

'You've done what?' I bent over him. 'Show me.'

'I landed on it,' he said, holding out

97

his hand to show me his middle finger, which was swelling alarmingly. 'But don't worry, I've sorted Tim out. He's gone off with Paul. Told you it would be OK.' He looked up at me, tried to smile and passed out.

I was still kneeling beside him on the garden path, when Dave put his head around the back door.

'Isobel, what's going on? Where's Tim?'

His expression changed as he saw Grandad. 'Is he OK?'

'He thinks he's broken a finger. He's lucky he didn't break his hips. The rosemary broke his fall. But don't worry, Tim's on his way to the church.' I could feel my voice cracking, half with hysteria, and Dave bounded down the step. 'I'll drop him at the hospital after I've taken Kelly and your dad to the church. Don't cry, Izzy.' He glanced at me. 'You'll wreck your make-up.'

'Such a romantic,' I snapped.

'I'm not going to hospital,' Grandad objected, sitting up groggily. 'Not before I've been to my granddaughter's wedding. Just get me out of this flower-bed. The smell's overpowering my aftershave.'

I could see Dad, silhouetted in the kitchen doorway, for once speechless.

'Give us a hand,' Dave called and, between them, they managed to haul Grandad to his feet. 'Can you bend your finger?' Dave asked.

'Course I can.' Grandad demonstrated and went white.

'Come and sit in the kitchen a minute,' I said. 'Dave, hadn't you better get changed?'

He shook his head and gave my father a quick, apologetic glance. 'No time. I'm going to have to go like this.'

Dad's eyes went involuntarily to his baseball cap.

'Well, not quite like this,' Dave amended, whipping it off and leaving it on the kitchen table.

'Taxi's here,' Mum called from the front door. 'Come on, everyone. We should have been there five minutes ago.'

★ ★ ★

The wedding photos were going to look very strange, I thought later, as I followed Kelly into the church. There'd be me in a grubby pink dress with a caterpillar of stitches above my lip. Grandad, wearing his favourite brown trousers, with earth stains down one leg, and Dave in his work jeans and black T-shirt. At least Mum and Dad were dressed for the part, although Mum had taken off her hat, having discovered one of Tim's aunts was wearing an identical one.

Kelly looked wonderful, though. Her dress fitted like a second skin, her face was radiant, if a little pale. She was like some beautiful ghost as she drifted down the aisle with Dad beside her. I wished I could see Tim's face as he took his vows, his voice low but sure. Mind you, I couldn't help thinking that if they'd got through this they could get through anything.

The service went without a hitch and then we were all traipsing out into the sunlight once more and the bells were pealing out their joyous song. Dave squeezed my hand. 'Made it,' he murmured, as we stood blinking in the sun, which shone brightly from a perfect blue sky, as if in defiance of everything else that had gone wrong.

'Never again am I getting involved in organising a wedding,' I whispered, as the photographer snapped away. But the words were hardly out of my mouth when Kelly glanced around, saw me, then picked up her dress and hurried across.

'Isobel, I'm not taking any chances with this one.' She handed me her bouquet and said, with a mischievous wink, 'It's your turn next.'

I took it graciously, aware that Dave was grinning at my side. Then Kelly added, in a voice only loud enough for me to hear, 'Tim guessed about the baby. I thought I'd binned the tester kit, but I left it on our bed. He's really pleased.'

'Great.' I smiled, but there wasn't time to say any more. The photographer was bossing everyone into groups.

'I don't think my finger's broken, after all,' Grandad said, when Dave tried to bully him into going to casualty. 'It's just a bit tattered. Anyway, I've had enough of hospitals.'

'I'll drive Kelly and Tim to the reception, if you like?' Dad said to Dave. 'Give you a chance to go and get changed.'

'You mean you don't want to take any more risks with your car,' Dave said. 'And you still don't approve of my dress sense?'

'Dave!' I said but, to my surprise Dad was smiling. He held out his hand and Dave took it.

'I misjudged you, son. You've got a lot of guts. Mind you, you need them, getting involved with this family.'

Dave didn't say anything, but I knew he was pleased.

Much later at the reception, when I figured Grandad had downed enough glasses of wine to tell me, I asked him what he'd said to Tim.

'Oh, nothing much. I knew all along that he wanted to marry Kelly. I just wanted to make sure that he knew he knew.'

'Run that by me again.'

'Well, he'd had a bit of a shock, hadn't he?' Grandad gave me a wink. 'The thing is, love, what you see depends on which angle you look at it from.' He bent his head close to the table. 'From down here the world looks completely different from up there. Well, it would if you could see anything in the first place.' He chuckled and took another gulp of wine.

'I think he's had too much to drink,' Dave whispered.

'Oh no, I haven't, young man.' Grandad frowned. 'I'll put it another way.' He hesitated. 'We all live in the same world. Agreed?'

We nodded.

'But we each see a different one. Your sister's world is full of drama. For Kelly, the whole world is a stage. Am I right or am I wrong?'

'Definitely right,' Dave conceded.

'Your father, Isobel, is like a cart-horse wearing blinkers. He never looks left or right. He only sees straight in front of him.'

I smiled. 'I don't think Dad would think much of that description.'

'He's got more of a sense of humour than you think.'

'He proved that just now,' Dave said. 'If I'd have said what I just said to him a couple of weeks ago, he'd have thumped me.'

'Ah, but he's had his blinkers ripped off, hasn't he?' Grandad hiccoughed. 'My finger feels enormously better now, I must say. Now, where did I get to? Ah yes, your mother. She's spent her whole life being a peacekeeper. Mothers do a lot of that. She spends her time diffusing situations.'

He was right, I thought. That was exactly what Mum did.

He turned towards Dave. 'And as for you, young man, the only thing clouding your vision is the past. Let go of it. Today's the only thing that's important.'

Dave looked flushed, but he was nodding, I saw, his eyes serious, as he reflected, no doubt, on his early years in an orphanage.

'What about me, Grandad?' I asked, suddenly curious. 'How do you think I see life?'

'Ah.' He put his head on one side and pretended to study me. 'I'd say that you're exactly the same as your sister — except that you're opposite sides of the same coin. She plays up every situation, while you play it down. You, Princess, make molehills out of mountains.'

'You still haven't told us what you said to Tim,' Dave reminded him.

'All I told Tim was that he should

forget whatever was clouding his vision right now. There was only one thing he ought to be considering. Did he love Kelly or did he not? If he did, then he should get on and marry her and they could sort everything else out later. If he didn't, then I said I'd call him a taxi.' He waved a hand and knocked his empty wineglass flying. 'Yes,' he said, 'my hand's better. That didn't hurt at all.'

About five minutes later he was asleep, his head lolling to one side, snoring gently. 'Fancy a dance?' Dave asked.

I nodded and we went on to the dance floor. The DJ, who seemed to have made a remarkable recovery from his bout of food poisoning, was playing Gareth Gates's *Unchained Melody*.

'We should do this more often,' Dave said, drawing me into his arms.

'Dance?'

'Come to weddings.' He grinned at my shocked expression. 'I know it took a lot of organising, but it was worth it in the end. Look at them.' He inclined his head towards Kelly and Tim, who were gazing into each other's eyes in the manner of deeply-in-love newly-weds. I smiled. Earlier on, Kelly had told me vehemently that there was no way we were going to pay for their honeymoon as we'd originally planned, but we could make a small contribution and spend the rest on ourselves.

'You deserve it,' she said. 'After everything I've put you both through lately.'

'I've had enough of weddings,' I said to Dave. 'Anyway, last week you said they were for traditionalists and romantics — not for sensible people like us.'

'Did I?' He raised his eyebrows and held me a little tighter. 'Well, maybe I've changed my mind. Your grandad may be drunk, but he's right. I do let the past cloud my life. It's about time I let go of it.'

'And that means you want to go to more weddings?' I kissed him. 'You big softie.'

'Well, not just any wedding. Ours.' He hesitated to let his words sink in. 'How about it, Isobel, will you marry me?'

'You've been drinking,' I accused, trying to suppress the little bubble of excitement inside me.

'Not enough to shlur my words.' He grinned. 'I mean it, Isobel. I love you and I want you to be my wife. If you like, we can wait a few days before telling your parents. Let them get over the shock of this wedding first.'

'I think that might be best,' I murmured, dipping my head and breathing in the wonderful, familiar scent of him.

'So is that a yes, then?'

He cupped my face in his hands so I couldn't look away and for a moment I gazed into the amazing depths of his eyes. 'It certainly is,' I said.

THE END

We do hope that you have enjoyed reading this large print book.

Did you know that all of our titles are available for purchase?

We publish a wide range of high quality large print books including:
Romances, Mysteries, Classics
General Fiction
Non Fiction and Westerns

Special interest titles available in large print are:
The Little Oxford Dictionary
Music Book, Song Book
Hymn Book, Service Book

Also available from us courtesy of Oxford University Press:
Young Readers' Dictionary
(large print edition)
Young Readers' Thesaurus
(large print edition)

For further information or a free brochure, please contact us at:
Ulverscroft Large Print Books Ltd.,
The Green, Bradgate Road, Anstey,
Leicester, LE7 7FU, England.
Tel: (00 44) 0116 236 4325
Fax: (00 44) 0116 234 0205

TRUTH, LOVE AND LIES

Valerie Holmes

Florence Swan's plan is to escape from Benford Mill School for young women before she is forced to work in their cotton mill. Naïve, ambitious and foolhardy, she ventures out on her own, her path crossing that of Mr Luke Stainbridge — a man accused of being mad. He has returned home from imprisonment in France to discover that his home has been claimed by an imposter. Together they find the truth, disproving clever lies, and discover life anew.

BITTERSWEET DECEPTION

Liz Fielding

Kate Thornley's catering business was suffering, so she unhesitatingly accepted the offer of a contract to set up a tearoom in the grounds of a stately home. However, if she'd known that media mogul Jason Warwick was to be her boss she would have turned it down flat. His devastating good looks ensured constant female attention. Kate wasn't interested in a temporary affair — and that was all he was offering. But could she defend herself against his seductive charm?

RETURN TO BUTTERFLY ISLAND

Rikki Sharp

After thirty years' absence, China Stuart returns to her birth place, the remote island of West Uist, to attend her aunt Beatrice's funeral — and finds she has inherited Stuart Grange. As if the funeral isn't traumatic enough, James McKriven, a land developer, is claiming the rights to China's ancestral home. Amongst the cobwebs and the cracked ceilings, China finds love, but faces the ghosts of the past . . . and the reason her family fled the island all those years ago.

A COLLECTOR OF HEARTS

Sally Quilford

It's 1936. Level-headed Caroline Conrad does not believe in ghosts, but even she is shaken when strange things start happening at a Halloween House Party. At Stony Grange Abbey, the atmosphere certainly unsettles her, but the presence of the handsome, albeit changeable, Blake Laurenson increases her sense of unease. Then Caroline finds herself fighting to clear her name. She's accused of stealing the priceless Cariastan Heart — has Blake framed her? And just who is the mysterious Prince Henri?

MEMORIES OF LOVE

Margaret Mounsdon

When Emily Sinclair discovers that deckchair attendant James Bradshaw is two-timing her with Madame Zora, she sprays the details in brilliant pink paint outside the fortune-teller's caravan. It's six years before Emily sees James again and she realises that she still loves him. The only trouble is, James has purchased the Victorian play house theatre she manages and, unless she can turn its fortune around, he is threatening to close it down.